398   c.1
No   Norman, Howard
    How Glooskap outwits the
    Ice Giants and other tales
    of the Maritime Indians

DATE DUE

OCT 25 '93			

Presented to
Mount Tamalpais
School Library

by

Mr. and Mrs. Glyn T.H. Ing
grandparents of
Christopher David Yahng '91
Kacie Elizabeth Yahng '94

How Glooskap Outwits the Ice Giants

and Other Tales of the Maritime Indians

RETOLD BY

HOWARD NORMAN

WOOD ENGRAVINGS BY

MICHAEL McCURDY

LITTLE, BROWN AND COMPANY

BOSTON TORONTO LONDON

for my nephew, Daniel — H.N.

Text Copyright © 1989 by Howard Norman
Illustrations Copyright © 1989 by Michael McCurdy

FIRST EDITION

The characters and events portrayed in this book are
fictitious. Any similarities to real persons, living or dead,
are coincidental and not intended by the author.

Several of these stories were published in slightly
different form in the *Boston Globe Magazine*.

Library of Congress Cataloging-in-Publication Data

Norman, Howard A.
   How Glooskap Outwits the Ice Giants / by Howard Norman;
illustrated by Michael McCurdy.
      p.   cm.
   "Joy Street books."
   Summary: Six tales featuring the mythical giant who roamed the
coast to New England and Canada, created the Indian peoples to keep
him company, and fought battles to protect them ever after.
   ISBN 0-316-61181-6
   1. Indians of North America — Maritime Provinces — Legends.
2. Indians of North America — New England — Legends. [1. Indians of
North America — Legends.] I. McCurdy, Michael, ill. II. Title.
III. Title: Glooskap the giant.
E78.M28N67   1989
398.2′08997 — dc19
[398.2]   89-2379
                                                                    CIP
                                                                     AC

        10   9   8   7   6   5   4   3   2   1
                        BP

Joy Street Books are published by
Little, Brown and Company (Inc.)

PRINTED IN THE UNITED STATES OF AMERICA

*Published simultaneously in Canada
by Little, Brown & Company (Canada) Limited*

Contents

▲▽▲

GLOOSKAP, in the Abenaki, Micmac, and other Indian languages of Maritime Canada and Maine, means "Man from Nothing," because he was considered the first person to inhabit the earth. He was a great hero and teacher. He taught people how they should live, about spiritual power, and how to overcome the obstacles that face mankind. According to legend, Glooskap traveled quite often from Nova Scotia, Canada, across the Bay of Fundy to what we now call New England; these tales relate what happened when he did.

How Glooskap Made
Human Beings

▲▼▲▼▲▼▲▼▲▼▽▲▽▲▽▲▽▲▽▽▲▽▲▽▲▽▲▽▲▽▲▽▲▽▲▽▲▽▲▼▲▼▲

Long, long ago the giant Glooskap began a journey. On a wild, stormy day he stepped into the Bay of Fundy. The waves and tides in the Bay of Fundy go in crazy directions. They even turn the water inside out! One minute the bay can be perfectly calm, the next a thousand waterspouts are spiraling over the surface and rainy winds are howling. Delighted with this challenge, Glooskap began to swim, and with a few strokes of his powerful arms, he traveled from Nova Scotia to the rocky shore of Maine.

For many years Glooskap enjoyed himself. He

walked through forests, climbed steep cliffs, paddled his canoe on lakes and rivers. He saw sleet, snow, hail, rain, sunshine, and every shape a cloud could take.

But one night, as he sat by his bonfire, he said to himself, "Something is wrong. I am lonely."

At that moment Glooskap got a brainstorm. "I'll create human beings!" he said excitedly.

But Glooskap worried that the world would be too dangerous for them. He had already made all the animals, and had made them giants like himself. Glooskap knew he'd have to solve this problem before he created human beings.

He thought up a plan.

"First," he said, "I'll question all the animals to find out how they might treat human beings."

The next morning, when Glooskap heard a moose bellowing in the distance, he got his first chance.

In five steps he reached the lake.

Slurping down lily pads by the dozens at the opposite shore was a moose, whose branching antlers cast a shadow over much of the lake.

"Ho, moose!" Glooskap hollered.

The moose looked up with astonishment. This was the first time he'd seen Glooskap, and the sight made him a little nervous.

"Ho, great Glooskap!" the moose called back. The moose's call caused a gale. Enormous waves crashed against Glooskap's legs, swirled trees up from their roots, and flipped boulders into the air.

"Easy does it!" Glooskap said. "I'll step closer so you don't have to shout."

"I'm surprised to see you," said the moose.

"Moose," Glooskap said seriously, "what would you do if human beings swam amid your lily pads?"

The moose munched lily pads and thought it over. "Do you intend to make these human beings giants like us?"

"No," said Glooskap.

"Then, to tell the truth," the moose said, "I'd dunk them under water, scoop them up with my antlers, and fling them as high as the geese fly!"

"Just as I feared!" Glooskap said, realizing that he'd made the moose far too strong.

He immediately spun the moose by his antlers, which was Glooskap's magic way of shrinking him.

Glooskap set the moose down. When his dizziness went away, the moose said, "It's strange being so much smaller! The trees are so tall!"

"You'll get used to it," Glooskap said.

Then Glooskap traveled around and made all the moose the size they are today.

It was grueling work. After he was finished, Glooskap slept for five days and nights in his cave by the sea.

When he woke, he decided to visit a forest of pine

trees. As he was walking, he saw a squirrel with hundreds of pine nuts stuffed into his cheeks.

"Ho, squirrel!" Glooskap called.

"Ho!" the squirrel answered, spitting pine nuts all over the forest. "I heard a rumor that you might create human beings!"

"Who'd you hear that from?" Glooskap asked.

"Moose," the squirrel said.

"Well, what you heard is true," said Glooskap. "So tell me, if human beings walked in your forest what would you do?"

The squirrel chewed furiously on a bunch of pine nuts, mulling over Glooskap's question. "To be honest," he finally said, "I'd bombard them with sharp pine needles, gnaw trees to come crashing down on them, and bury them in the ground with all the pine nuts I save for winter!"

"Just as I feared!" Glooskap exclaimed. "You are too strong!"

Glooskap took the squirrel in his hands and smoothed him down until he was the size that squirrels are today. Then Glooskap traveled to every forest and made all the squirrels smaller.

It was hard work. Once again Glooskap went to his cave by the sea. He slept for a week.

But a rumbling growl loud as thunder woke him.

In those days, there were great white bears. They liked to lie on their backs in cool tidal pools and sunbathe all day long. They were the laziest animals on earth. With one huge paw they could flip a hundred salmon into the air and gulp them down all at once! Whereupon their day's work would be done.

Glooskap peered out of his cave down the cliff to the beach. There sat a great white bear.

"Ho, lazy bear!" Glooskap called down.

The bear's tracks on the beach were the size of ponds.

"Ho, Glooskap!" the bear growled.

"Bear," said Glooskap, "did you talk to a squirrel recently?"

"As a matter of fact," the bear replied, "I did. The squirrel told me you might create human beings."

"That's right," said Glooskap, "and I'd like to know what you'd do if human beings fished for salmon in the sea."

The bear stood up to full size, so that he was face-to-face with Glooskap, opened his mouth, which was as wide as Glooskap's cave, and said, "With my paw I'd flip them into the air and devour them without even thinking twice!"

"Just as I thought!" Glooskap said. He immediately pressed down on the bear until he was the size that polar bears are today. "Now," said Glooskap, "go off and live among the glaciers and ice storms where you'll have to work hard to make a living!"

Glooskap then shrunk all the great white bears and banished them to the far north.

Shrinking great white bears was no easy task. Glooskap was worn out. He returned to his cave; this time he slept for two weeks.

When he woke, Glooskap decided to continue his journeying. But he didn't want to travel alone. So he chose two wolves, one black, one white, as companions. Everywhere Glooskap went, the wolves were by his side.

So it was that Glooskap went all over the earth, questioning the giant animals — beaver, fox, coyote, eagle, turtle, seal, and sea gull. The animals were headstrong and mischievous, and all told Glooskap what harm they would do to human beings, if they had the chance. So, using all sorts of magic, Glooskap changed them all to the size they are today. He worked hard for many years until, finally, he felt that human beings would be safe on the earth.

"Now," Glooskap announced, "it is time for me to make human beings."

The animals of the forest crowded around. "What I'm about to do," Glooskap said, "is mysterious."

Glooskap used a powerful magic that he had saved for this moment. He waved his arms, smoke flew up from the ground, there was a blinding light so that the animals had to throw themselves to the ground, covering their eyes.

They were afraid.

But when they next looked up, they burst into laughter.

They saw human beings setting out in all directions: north, south, east, and west.

"Look!" a bear shouted, "they walk on two feet!"

The animals were delighted with their new companions on the earth. "Human beings are quite an invention!" a wolf shouted. "Glooskap, you have a great sense of humor!"

And that is what happened when animals first saw human beings.

How Glooskap Outwits
the Ice Giants

After a long rest in his cave by the sea, Glooskap wanted to see the people he had created. He wanted to know what sort of houses they lived in, what they ate, how they treated each other, and what they feared.

He walked along the coast of Maine until he heard a strange sound. He stopped to listen carefully. In the near distance through the trees, the Indian people in a village were sighing. Their sighs sounded like a breeze rustling through dry leaves.

Glooskap walked to this village of sighs. The people

there lived in wooden huts. When they saw Glooskap, they stopped sighing and welcomed him with a magnificent feast — they cooked soups and stews in big pots and fried dozens of fish over a fire. A visit from Glooskap might happen only once in a lifetime, and they celebrated with singing and dancing. They gave Glooskap woven baskets, deer-horn rattles, blankets, feather garments, and the most special gifts of all, spirit-masks, which were like the wild, beautiful, and fierce faces that come to people only in dreams.

When the feast had ended, Glooskap said, "I am most impressed with your celebration, but what about the sighs I heard? There must be something you fear."

The chief stepped forward and said, "Yes — we fear the Ice Giants."

"Tell me about these Ice Giants," Glooskap said.

Everyone hushed as the chief spoke. "The Ice Giants," he said, "are powerful wizards. They live in a nearby village. No one dares go near it. There is a father Ice Giant, his two sons, and a daughter. They travel a great deal. They just say, 'Let's begin walking,' and off they go. They carry nothing with them and are gone for days at a time. When they travel, we stop sighing. When they are at home, we sigh with fear and sadness."

The chief began to tremble. He grew quiet.

"What's the matter?" Glooskap asked. "Why did you stop?"

"There is something so horrible," the chief said, "that I hardly dare speak of it."

"You must," said Glooskap, "if I am to help you."

The chief took a deep breath, then said, "The village of the Ice Giants is scattered with human bones."

When Glooskap glanced around the village he saw that each and every person was afraid. They were looking over their shoulders, as though the Ice Giants themselves might stomp in at any moment!

"What have you done so far about these Ice Giants?" Glooskap asked.

The chief merely shrugged his shoulders and sighed. "What can we do? Whenever an Ice Giant wants to, it steals one of us," the chief said. "In the morning there is one less person in our village. Everything the Ice Giants do is cruel. But we are helpless against their strength."

"I must do something about this!" Glooskap said. "I knew those Ice Giants when they were young. They didn't eat human beings back then. Yet I know what you have told me is the truth, so I will have to use my powers against the Ice Giants. Whoever hurts human beings, I will fight. It makes no difference if they are giants like myself!"

Glooskap scanned the horizon in every direction. From his great height, he saw that the Ice Giants had moved up the coast to the Bay of Fundy. They had made camp on a sandbar in the middle of a river.

Glooskap snuck as quietly as a giant could to the trees by the river, crouched in hiding, and spied on the Ice Giants. He saw that the father of the Ice Giants was one-eyed and half gray.

Glooskap decided to play a trick.

He made himself one-eyed and half gray, too! He entered the Ice Giants' hut and sat down next to the old man.

Outside the hut, the Ice Giant brothers heard someone talking. They were curious, and slyly looked in and saw the newcomer. "He looks just like Father," one said. "Our father never mentioned that he had a twin," the other said. "This must be an imposter! He's trying to act as if he's part of our family. We have to do something about this."

But the Ice Giant's daughter took up a whale's tail and cooked it for the stranger. She placed it on newly peeled birch bark and put it in front of him. The stranger had just taken a bite, when an Ice Giant brother rushed in, full of rage and jealousy. "You never fed me delicious whale's tail!" he said to his sister. Then he snatched up the birch bark and ran off with the rest of the whale's tail.

Glooskap said, "The Ice Giants first offer me a meal, then take it back. I'll have to retrieve it for myself!"

Glooskap did not leave the hut, though. He sat still. He closed his eyes and wished the whale's tail back to him. And back it came on the newly peeled birch bark, right into Glooskap's hands!

The Ice Giants huddled together and watched in amazement. Finally, the father said, "This, truly, is a great wizard in our midst. But to find out just how great, we'll test him further."

An Ice Giant brother raced from the hut and soon returned, lugging a huge whale's jawbone. He set the jawbone upright on the ground. Gripping it tightly with both hands, leaning all his weight into it, he tried to break the jawbone, but it bent only a little. He then turned to Glooskap and said, "You try it."

Using only his thumb, Glooskap snapped it like a pipestem!

Again the Ice Giants agreed. "He is a very great wizard, but to see how great we must test him still further."

The Ice Giant father said, "Let's play a game of ball!"

Glooskap said, "Agreed. I'll provide the ball."

He went over to a tree near the river, broke off a bough, and turned it into a skull, more hideous than anything the Ice Giants had ever seen. The Ice Giants fled!

Glooskap was seldom one to boast, but he was so pleased to have outwitted the Ice Giants that he stomped on the ground. Foaming water rushed down from the mountains. All the earth rang with the roar. Glooskap then sang a magical song, and quick as

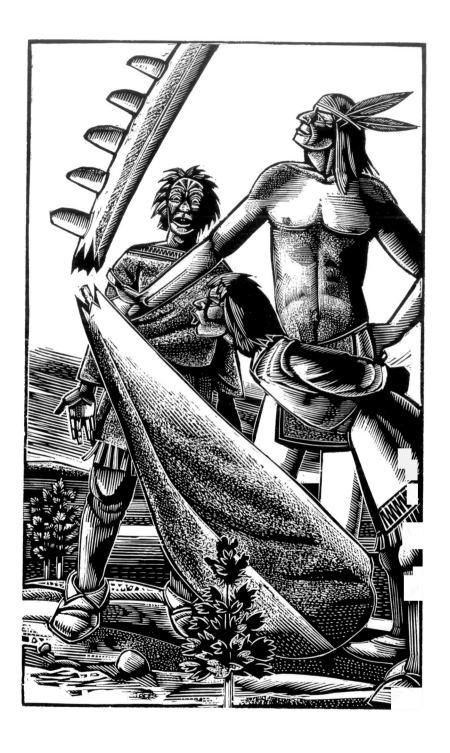

lightning he became Glooskap the giant again. He sang a second song, which changed the fleeing Ice Giants into fish, each as long as a man. They flopped into the river rapids and swam to the sea, to live there forever.

Every once in a while they would surface just to have a look at Glooskap on shore, picking his teeth with a splintered piece of whale's jawbone.

And back in the village of sighs, the people were no longer afraid.

Why the Sea Winds
Are the Strength
They Are Today

Glooskap liked to sit on the sand dunes and watch his Indian friends in their canoes. They were excellent paddlers and could go far out to sea. Once in a while a whale would spout, its enormous body rolling like a black wave over the sea. Its broadly fanned tail would slap down, spraying the Indians with foam. The canoes would rock on the swells. If one was tossed and capsized, Glooskap would right it, then pluck the Indians up and set them in it, handing them the paddles.

And if Glooskap saw the dark, roiling clouds and slanting rain of a storm blowing in, he would call out,

"Storm! Storm!" He would catch the jagged lightning bolts in midair. He would guide the canoes to safety.

But in those days there lived a giant, fearsome bird, whom the Indians called Wuchowsen. His name meant "He-Who-Causes-Ferocious-Storms." Wuchowsen sat on a boulder by the sea. Whenever he rustled his wings, clacked his beak, or scratched himself with a talon, a tremendous storm started up! He caused gales, hurricanes, and lashing hailstorms that rushed in so quickly that even Glooskap had no time to warn the Indians.

One day Glooskap went to watch the Indians race in their canoes. But when he reached the sand dunes, he found a dozen canoes washed up and splintered on the beach. One look and he knew that many Indian people had drowned. Glooskap let out a mournful, echoing cry. "Wuchowsen, I know you have done this terrible thing!"

Just then, Glooskap saw a shadow glide over the sand. He looked up to see the grinning Wuchowsen flying past, each flap of his wings as loud as thunder. "Here is a gift just for you, Glooskap," Wuchowsen called.

Whoosh! Suddenly Glooskap himself was swirled up into the air by a tornado of sand. It spun him along the beach, then flung him against some boulders. This was followed by a storm that lasted for five days, and carried with it the most brutal winds Glooskap had ever experienced. He crouched in his cave as the wind howled outside like a thousand wolves.

"I must find that Wuchowsen!" Glooskap said. Northward along the coast, toppled trees and boulders stacked in strange formations marked the storm's trail. Glooskap followed it until he found Wuchowsen sitting on his boulder, daydreaming of storms.

"Wuchowsen!" Glooskap said with anger. "You have no mercy on people. You move your wings, clack your beak, and scratch with your talons a little too often!"

The giant bird answered, "I have lived on this earth as long as you have, Glooskap! I have sat on this boulder for centuries. In the old days, I flapped my wings and clacked whenever I wanted to! Storms are my life! I'll do as I please!"

But Glooskap rose up to his full size and flew high into the sky, taking Wuchowsen with him as if he were just a little duck.

Far above the clouds, Glooskap tied Wuchowsen's wings together and threw him down onto the rocks.

Now there were calm seas for many years, and the Indian people could go out in their canoes all day long, without fear of being ambushed by Wuchowsen's dreaded storms. But gradually the water became stagnant. It grew thick and mucky. The whales fled far out to sea, where mud did not get into their spouts, and where they could swim freely.

"We need a storm to break up these waters," Glooskap

declared. "Why, I can't even paddle my magic canoe through them."

Glooskap remembered Wuchowsen. "Maybe I shouldn't have been so rough on him," he said. Glooskap searched and searched, and finally found Wuchowsen right where he had always lived, on his boulder by the sea. Wuchowsen's broken bones had mended, and his wounds had healed. But his wings were still tied and only rustled ever so lightly, causing just a slight breeze. Only the tiniest twigs were flipped into the air; only minnows were slapped to shore.

"Wuchowsen," Glooskap said, "I am glad to see you are still alive. I'm giving you one more chance. We need your help in clearing the waters."

Glooskap approached carefully, untied one of Wuchowsen's wings — and immediately a sharp wind knocked Glooskap on his back! As he lay on the ground, he heard a thunderclap and saw a pack of black clouds tumbling.

Glooskap stood up and brushed himself off. "I see you haven't lost your skills!" he said, laughing.

"Just untie my other wing," Wuchowsen said. "Then I'll brew up a storm that will last a hundred years!"

"I think not," Glooskap said. "I will keep one of your wings tied forever. Now, cause a storm that clears the waters, and nothing more. Or I will bind up both your wings again!"

Glooskap went the length of the coast in ten leaps,

arriving at the Indian village. He said, "A storm is approaching," and as he spoke, the first squalls appeared on the horizon. Quickly, the people secured their huts. As the storm raged, they huddled inside. The thunder drummed in their ears. Their huts creaked and leaned in the wind. But all through this Glooskap stood guard, batting away jagged lightning and swallowing tidal waves.

When the weather finally cleared, the waters were running free; whales lolled about not far from shore. The sun had broken through.

The storm had scattered the Indian canoes every which way; finding each and every one, Glooskap lined them up on the beach. "Why not spend a day out at sea?" he said. And that is exactly what the Indian people did.

And every now and then, Glooskap visits the giant bird, Wuchowsen, just to make sure one wing is still bound tightly.

Glooskap Gets Two Surprises

One morning Glooskap sat on his favorite sand dune and looked at the sea. Sun glinted off a thousand whitecaps. Indian people bathed in the shallows and fished from canoes in deeper water. Gulls keened overhead, and cliff swallows somersaulted in the air, chasing the wind.

"I'm in a good mood today," Glooskap said. "A very, very good mood."

Just when he had said this, the chief of a nearby village ran up. "Glooskap," he said, "I'm afraid I have horrible news."

"Nothing can trouble me today," Glooskap said. *"Nothing."*

"Every wicked magician, every cunning sorcerer, every ghost, every fiend, every cannibal, every goblin, and every treacherous beast are meeting right now," the chief said, trembling.

"How rude of them!" Glooskap laughed. "They didn't even invite me!"

"Don't you want to know what the meeting is about?" said the chief.

"Oh, most certainly," said Glooskap. "Forgive me, yes, go on, tell me."

"They are plotting to do away with you!" the chief said.

Glooskap's smile turned into a frown so quickly, it was almost as if the world itself had turned upside-down.

"I knew you would be angry," the chief said.

Glooskap stomped on the ground, so that the chief had to hold his hands over his ears; it was like being in an earthquake. "Me? Angry?" said Glooskap. "No, I'm not angry!" He stomped some more, kicked a few boulders into the sea, yanked at his hair, sat down, and scowled.

The chief went back to his village.

Glooskap sat brooding. "All the magicians, sorcerers, ghosts, fiends, cannibals, goblins, and beasts are jealous of my great powers," he said to himself. "I've known this for a long time. But now their jealousy has turned evil, and I must tend to this matter quickly."

Glooskap walked to a rocky field. He got down on his knees, put an ear to the ground, and listened. He heard his enemies plotting to do away with him. He heard magicians clicking long knives together, sorcerers bubbling up a poisonous soup in a cauldron. He heard fiends, ghosts, cannibals, and goblins practicing magic songs to pierce Glooskap's ears — oh, they had hideous, cackling voices! He heard beasts filing and whittling their teeth into harpoons.

Suddenly Glooskap heard one fiend say, "It is time. Let us go get Glooskap."

But Glooskap had a plan.

He pushed aside some large rocks, then reached down into the earth, his arm making a tunnel to the magicians, sorcerers, fiends, ghosts, cannibals, goblins, and beasts.

When Glooskap drew his arm back, his enemies looked up and saw his face. Glooskap grinned. He leaned down, put his mouth over the tunnel's entrance, and hollered, "Ha! Ha, ha, ha, ha, ha, ha, ha, ha!" Then he guffawed, "Guffaw, guffaw, guffaw, guffaw, guffaw, guffaw!"

Glooskap's laughter filled the tunnel. The sound made his enemies writhe with pain. They stuffed dirt into their ears, but the laughter pierced straight through and echoed inside their heads! Glooskap laughed and laughed, until the magicians, sorcerers, fiends, ghosts, cannibals, goblins, and beasts could hardly stand it. With one, final laugh — Ha! — an avalanche smothered Glooskap's enemies.

Now there was a vast silence, the kind of silence that arrives only after Glooskap has stopped laughing and an avalanche has settled to a mere trickle of dirt and pebbles.

"Now," boasted Glooskap, "there is no one or nothing that can overpower me!"

"Are you certain, Master Glooskap?" Glooskap heard someone say, in a lovely voice.

He turned around and saw a beautiful woman.

"What do you mean, am I certain?" said Glooskap.

"I think there is still at least one who remains unconquered," the woman said.

In some surprise Glooskap said, "What is the name of this mighty one?"

"He is called Wasis," replied the woman, "but I strongly advise you to keep away from him."

"How dare you!" Glooskap cried. "The great Glooskap is afraid of no one!"

"Be careful. This one is quite different," the woman warned.

"Begone with you!" Glooskap ordered, and the woman ran away.

The very next day Glooskap encountered this Wasis. When he saw Wasis, he laughed to himself. "So *this* is the unconquerable Wasis!" he said, for Wasis was only a baby. He sat on the ground sucking on a piece of maple sap and humming a song. Glooskap had spent little time around children as small as Wasis, but with perfect confidence he smiled at the baby and beckoned him. The baby smiled back, but did not budge.

"When Glooskap calls," Glooskap said, "you hurry to him!"

But the baby ignored Glooskap, and went on sucking the candy and humming.

This confounded Glooskap, but then he thought, "Aha! I know a way to draw this baby nearer. I'll imitate wild and beautiful birdsongs. No one can resist that!" Glooskap chirped, whistling long and lovely notes and making whispering coos.

Still, Wasis paid Glooskap no attention. Looking bored, he threw his maple candy at Glooskap. It stuck to Glooskap's foot.

Glooskap was not used to being disobeyed. He stomped and yanked his hair, and said, "If you don't crawl over here, I'll throw you into the sea!" Glooskap then made all sorts of other threats, all the while flailing at a pine tree until its branches fell all around Wasis.

Wasis wrinkled up his face. "Waaahhh!" he cried. "Waaahhh! Waaahhh!" He wailed louder and louder, until Glooskap covered his ears and tossed himself to the ground. "I've never heard such a bloodcurdling screech!" he said.

Glooskap summoned all his magic resources to try and quiet down Wasis. He cast his mightiest spells, shouted his most dreadful curses, recited his ancient chants, and sang his wildest songs loud enough to raise the dead.

But Wasis only cried more loudly.

Finally, as Glooskap fled in frustration and despair, Wasis stopped his crying, smiled, and looked amused. He softly said, "Ga ga ga ga goo," the way all babies talk.

This is how Glooskap got two surprises.

And it is how he threw a tantrum, and got one thrown back at him.

How Magic Friend Fox
Helped Glooskap
against the Panther-Witch

One day, meandering back to his cave by the sea, Glooskap stopped at an Indian village. As always, the people there were pleased to see him. They fed him an abundance of fish, moose meat, and rabbits. After his meal, Glooskap noticed there were only two children in the village, a girl and a boy. "Where are all the children?" he asked in alarm.

The village chief said, "It is the she-panther Pukjinsk-west. She's been prowling. At night she throws a magic cloak over the moon, then scratches a boulder with her claws and screams loud enough to split any tree.

Then — suddenly — it gets deathly quiet. That's when we truly worry. And in the morning, we discover that Pukjinskwest has stolen another child!"

Pukjinskwest was a giant cat, with fangs like icicles. Long ago she learned to fly to the moon; there she put moonlight into her eyes so that they shone brightly in the dark.

"The last time I visited the moon," Glooskap said, "Pukjinskwest was living there with her twin scissorbill birds."

"I'm afraid she's returned," the chief said.

Pukjinskwest's constant companions were two scissorbill birds. They hovered above the sea rocks, looking for mermaids. They would swoop down, pluck up a mermaid, and snip her in half. Then they would sit on the rocks, crunching the mermaid's bones. It was hard to know who was more nasty, Pukjinskwest or her birds.

Not only did Pukjinskwest want to kidnap all the Indian children, she wanted to replace Glooskap as chief of all the Indians. But Glooskap promised his people that these things would not happen. "Never," he said, "not as long as I'm here!"

Glooskap knew that Pukjinskwest loved to eat children. But he knew she also found turtle eggs delectable. She had a favorite island where she hoarded the eggs. Her scissorbill birds would fly her there. Glooskap knew where this island was.

He paddled his canoe there and began searching for

her supply of eggs. He knew that this would anger Pukjinskwest. After a while, her scissorbills clacked overhead, and began dropping mermaid bones on him. But Glooskap put on a hat, and the bones ricocheted off.

Glooskap dug all day in the scorching sun, but found only sand and roots. "Egg hunting is hard work, especially if you can't find any!" he said. He grew tired and sat under a shade tree to take a nap. Just as he fell asleep, the scissorbills lifted his magic canoe into the air and delivered it to Pukjinskwest, who had been hiding in a gulch and gorging on turtle eggs.

Quickly, Pukjinskwest bounded to the beach with the canoe, and began to paddle toward the mainland. "I'm leaving this island," she sang, "and I'm going to be chief!"

When she arrived at the mainland, she ran to the nearest Indian village. "Glooskap is dead," she announced. "I am the new chief!"

"That's impossible," one of the Indians said with a laugh.

"Seize him!" Pukjinskwest ordered her scissorbills. The birds nabbed the Indian and quickly bit him in half.

The villagers gasped and wept. They threw rocks at Pukjinskwest, but the scissorbills batted them away.

"Anyone who protests," Pukjinskwest warned, "will meet the same fate."

For days and weeks and months the villagers waited

for Glooskap to return. "Why doesn't he just leap back to the mainland?" they wondered aloud. "Maybe he's abandoned us!" The villagers were confused. Pukjinskwest remained as chief, and life was sorrowful.

The village began to fill with mermaid bones.

On the island, Glooskap said, "Pukjinskwest is one of the slyest, most powerful enemies I have ever faced. It has taken me a long time to puzzle out a special plan to outwit her, but finally I have!" Glooskap closed his eyes and wished for his friend the fox to come to the island. When he opened his eyes, the fox was in front of him.

"What secret do you know about Pukjinskwest?" Glooskap asked the fox.

"I know that she cannot swim," the fox said. "She is terribly afraid of water and even has nightmares of drowning in the sea. That is why she either crosses to the island in a canoe, or orders her scissorbills to carry her. Their talons are strong, and they could never drop her, no matter how rough the winds."

"Very good," Glooskap said. "I knew I could count on you. Now go to the village and tell Pukjinskwest that you have used your magic on her behalf. Say that you have filled this island with turtle eggs. She won't be able to resist."

The fox did as Glooskap had requested. He used his magic to fly to the mainland, then ran to the village. When Pukjinskwest saw the fox, she was suspicious.

She knew that Glooskap and the fox were old friends. Still, she bragged, "Look around you, fox. See how I am in control here. Don't try any of your fox tricks, because my scissorbills are right behind you!"

The fox heard a horrible clacking and turned around to find the scissorbills, with their dull eyes, shabby feathers, and scaly legs, close by. The fox was truly afraid, but he was brave, too, and went ahead with Glooskap's plan. "No," he said to Pukjinskwest, "I wouldn't think of using my tricks. In fact, I've come to tell you some good news."

"What is it?" asked Pukjinskwest.

"Your favorite island is now loaded with thousands of turtle eggs. I have made it so!"

"That's as it should be," Pukjinskwest said. "Everyone should bestow fine gifts on the chief of all the Indians — me! And do you know what your reward will be?"

"Pray tell," said the fox.

"You shall have all the mermaid bones you can carry!" said Pukjinskwest.

The fox gulped. "Thank you," he said. "Mermaid bones are what I've always wanted!"

The fox dragged off some bones, which he gently cast off one by one into the sea, hoping the mermaid spirits would be happy to have their bones returned.

That night, Pukjinskwest dreamed of turtle eggs, as

usual. She lay on her mattress suffed with mermaid bones, growling with delight. Then, she woke up and walked to the sea, with her moonlit eyes shining out ahead as her guide. The sea was very wild; the waves crashed against the cliffs. But Pukjinskwest couldn't get the eggs out of her mind. "I will summon my scissorbills to fly me to the island, where I'll feast all night," she said.

Just then, she heard a voice. "It is I, the fox. I'll take you across on my back, Mistress Pukjinskwest. It would be an honor."

"Well, all right," said Pukjinskwest. "But swim strongly and swiftly, and go directly to the island."

Pukjinskwest climbed upon the fox's back and the fox began to swim with sure strokes toward the island. "Please," he said to Pukjinskwest, "draw in your claws, for they are making deep scratches in my back."

Pukjinskwest drew in her talon-claws and said, "How much farther is the island?"

Instead of replying, the fox rose into the air and spilled the panther-witch into the roiling sea!

"I can't swim!" Pukjinskwest cried out.

"Who is the chief of all the Indians?" the fox asked from up in the air.

"I am — Pukjinskwest!" the she-cat shouted. But then she sank below the surface. When she bobbed up again, the fox saw that the water had doused her eyes. They hissed like wet coals.

"I think you are mistaken," the fox said. "I ask again: Who is chief of all the Indians?"

"It is Pukjinskwest who is chief!" the panther-witch replied. But then her fearful growl turned to a gargling purr, as seawater filled her throat.

"One more time I will ask you: Who is the chief of all the Indians?" the fox said.

Pukjinskwest knew that she was about to drown. With a last choking gasp she said, "Glooskap — the great Glooskap is chief of all the Indians."

"Did you hear that?" the fox called out into the darkness.

"Yes," said Glooskap. "I was listening the whole time."

"Shall I deliver Pukjinskwest to the moon now?" asked the faithful fox.

"Yes," said Glooskap, "do that very thing."

So it was that the magic fox flew the panther-witch Pukjinskwest back to her lair on the moon. Glooskap then leapt to the mainland and went to the Indian village. "I have outwitted Pukjinskwest," he said with pride. And he resumed his life as chief of all the Indians.

Now Pukjinskwest lives on the moon without turtle eggs, without children to devour. She whimpers and is a mangy sight. She lives alone, because her scissor-bill birds choked to death on mermaid bones. The magic fox saw to that. She has never forgotten her grudge against Glooskap, but there is nothing she can do about it.

Once in a while Glooskap stands on a cliff by the sea, places his hands together to make a telescope, and peers up at the moon. There he sees the moon-hermit Pukjinskwest, sitting on her raft made of mermaid bones, in the middle of a waterless crater.

How Glooskap Sang
through the Rapids
and Found a New Home

As time went on, Glooskap grew weary of saving people from nasty creatures and listening to their woes. He loved people, but did not wish to live around them all the time. "I want to be only as tall as any Indian man," he decided. "I want a secluded house by a river, where I can live in peace and quiet, well away from the troubles of the world."

Glooskap summoned his wolves, whom he had not seen in many years. "We are going on a long journey," he told them. "It must be kept a secret. I don't want people to see me unhappy."

"What is our destination?" the wolves asked.

"I can tell you what I want," said Glooskap, "but I can't tell you *where*. I want you both to fly to every corner of the earth. Find me a house to live in. It must be near a river, where fish are plentiful and nobody will come to me with their woes. Things are fine in the world now, the creatures who would harm mankind are all dead or on the moon. It is up to people to take care of themselves. I need a rest."

The wolves flew off and were gone for a year. Glooskap waited in his cave.

Finally, the two wolves returned. "We have found your house," they said. "But it is not a simple matter to get to it."

"Let's go," Glooskap said happily, "I've been waiting. I'm ready."

The wolves led Glooskap to a river he had never seen before. On the sandy bank was his canoe. "Old friend," he said to the canoe, "we have been through many adventures together. Now we are about to go through yet another."

Glooskap climbed in. He tied each of his wolves to a canoe slat. He took up his oar and started downstream. The day was clear and sunny, the water was calm, with only harmless whirlpools and ripples in the shallows. Glooskap glided his canoe along with little effort.

"Why not practice your wild-rapids song?" the wolves suggested. "It is your most powerful song."

"Look around you," Glooskap said, with a wide sweep of his hand. "There's no need for my rapids song."

"This is a strange and powerful river," the wolves warned Glooskap. "We traveled on it for many days. We almost drowned in this river. It has many deceptions. It plays many tricks."

"Pipe down," Glooskap said, laughing. "I'm enjoying my escape from the worries of mankind."

Glooskap closed his eyes and let the river breeze wash over his face. He leaned back and let his canoe drift with the current.

But when he opened his eyes, Glooskap saw ten vultures circling above. "Am I dead?" he asked his wolves. "Have I died and am I traveling to the land of ghosts and bones?"

"No," said one wolf, "those are death-birds all right, but you have not died, great Glooskap. Those vultures are waiting for us to collide into jagged rocks and capsize. They are waiting for us to wash ashore, so they can land on our faces and tear us apart with their beaks."

"But I see no jagged rocks!" said Glooskap.

"Please," the wolves begged, "sing your wild-rapids song."

"No," said Glooskap, "I'm enjoying the view. You

wolves worry far too much. You've got to learn to enjoy life."

"The house we picked out is truly peaceful," one wolf replied. "We will enjoy life greatly once we are there."

"Sing me a song," Glooskap said. "If you insist on singing, *you* sing. Make it a song of great enthusiasm. A song of quiet waters, and no vultures in the sky."

"All right," said the wolves, "we will sing."

But when the wolves began to sing, they sang Glooskap's wild-rapids song! They howled it with great fear in their hearts.

Glooskap was annoyed. "Stop!" he said, "that's *my* song! That's my most magical song. Only I can sing it. You're ruining the song!"

"Teach us, then," the wolves pleaded.

With much pride, Glooskap puffed out his chest, took a deep breath, and sang his powerful wild-rapids song. The song had in it the names of every Indian and animal who had ever drowned. As he sang, Glooskap noticed a peculiar thing. With each name in the song, a new vulture appeared in the sky!

Finally, the vultures were so numerous that they blocked out the sun.

Now even Glooskap grew worried.

When the sun vanished entirely behind this thick cloud of vultures, Glooskap and his wolves suddenly found themselves amid towering cliffs. The cliffs closed in on them, and the river rushed them toward thundering white-water rapids just up ahead. Glooskap clung to his wolves. Even his magic canoe felt flimsy in the turbulence. Every so often the sun flashed through a vulture's wing feathers, reflecting off the rocks and blinding Glooskap. "What is going on?" Glooskap cried.

"Sing your rapids song!" the wolves shouted. "Sing! Sing!"

The canoe slid forward into a treacherous gulch. The churning of the rapids became so loud that Glooskap could not even hear his own singing. The canoe jumped and spun sideways, then tumbled down a waterfall, which led to a second waterfall, then a third, a fourth, and a fifth. "We are falling off the world!" Glooskap thought, but he did not say it. He sang as loudly as he could.

They landed below the last waterfall, and saw up ahead an even more menacing sight. Protruding from the turbulent rapids were rocks that stood like pointy teeth!

Glooskap could hear the wolves' hearts pounding with wild alarm.

"Glooskap," the wolves said, "close your eyes and imagine a well-built house. It is made of logs and there is a fire in the fireplace and a good meal on the table. Life there is peaceful, terrible rapids are only a memory."

Glooskap tightly closed his eyes. "I see it!" he said. "I see my house! And you are right there with me, my wolves!"

"Now sing, Glooskap!" the wolves said. "Sing as you have never sung before. Sing from all your experiences, from all your adventures, from all your days on the earth!"

Glooskap sang.

And suddenly, the canoe passed through the dangerous ravine and out into the sunlight. The river here was cold and deep, and the speckled stones that lay at the bottom had traveled as far as Glooskap and his wolves had. Glooskap peered into the water and said to the stones, "I feel like I have known you my whole life."

"Look!" the wolves said.

Glooskap shaded his eyes from the sun and saw his house, there on a knoll not far from the riverbank. "It is just as you described it," he said to the wolves. And he began to weep.

Since that day many people have tried to find Glooskap's house, but Glooskap and his wolves are the only ones who know where it is. There is no map to Glooskap's house.

Glooskap is happy. He spends his days fishing and running with his wolves. At night, after supper, Glooskap and his wolves talk of their adventures.

"We have done much good," Glooskap likes to say.

Glooskap is the size of any Indian man now, that is true. But if one of his wolves should venture far and wide, returning with the news that mankind is in trouble, he will become a giant again, and will hazard the mystical river with his wolves in order to help his people.